The
Endless
Pavement

For Karen --

Up with feet!

Jacqueline Jackson

Bill Perlmutter

The Endless Pavement

JACQUELINE JACKSON
and WILLIAM PERLMUTTER

Illustrated by Richard Cuffari

The Seabury Press
New York

The Endless Pavement was presented in rough draft in Springfield, Illinois, April, 1971, at a symposium "A Futuristic Children's Book in Progress" during Sangamon State University's University Week, "The Year 2001." The authors thank Sangamon State, and the many participants in the symposium who gave critiques, ideas, and encouragement.

Designed by Judith Lerner
Printed in the United States of America

Library of Congress Cataloging in Publication Data

Jackson, Jacqueline.
    The endless pavement.

    SUMMARY: Living in a time when people are the servants of automobiles and ruled by the master auto of the planet, Josette longs to leave her rollabout and try her legs.
    [1. Fantasy.   2. Science fiction]   I. Perlmutter, William, Joint author.   II. Title.
PZ7.J13617En   [Fic]   73-7130
ISBN 0-8164-3105-1

TO JOSETTE,
GREG, AND ELSPETH,
WHOSE LEGS
HAVE NOT (YET)
TURNED INTO WHEELS

IN A red-and-white striped
Home-a-rolla
that never stopped going
lived Josette with her father and mother.
At nine every morning
the Home-a-rolla in its home lane
and the School-a-rolla
in its service lane
stopped across from each other
and Josette scooted down one ramp
and up another
to her classroom
(for even children were bolted
into their own single rollabouts
from the time they could sit up
and twirl a steering wheel).

When the opening horn blew
she looked up at the Screen
where the master auto of the planet,
the greatest of the great autos,
the Great Computer-mobile,
with its chrome grill
its retractable top
and beaming headlights,
led them in the pledge:

"I pledge allegiance
To the great autos
And to the concrete on which they roll;
One pavement, under Ford, indivisible,
With mobility and power steering
For all."

Then she snapped out her Teach-UR-Self kit,
arranged her tools on her work tray,
and spent the day silently practicing
tightening lug nuts
testing the circuitry on
electro-magnetic cutoff jets
and bolting plenum tubes
until the closing horn sounded.

8

She recited with her classmates,

"The travel lanes goeth toward the South
And returneth to the North;
They circleth about continually
And returneth again
To their beginnings,"

and then she snapped her Teach-UR-Self kit
into the wall where it would be scanned
during the night,
pushed in her work tray,
released her spring steering wheel,
raised her windshield,
and was ready to roll
to meet her mother
and the red-and-white Home-a-rolla
at the ramp.

Every afternoon
when she got home from school
Josette liked to watch
the green-and-pink Ranch-a-rolla
behind them which had rolled along there

as long as she could remember.
Once the little boy who lived in it
had started to print something
on the windshield
with a calorie stick
but his mother, who was driving,
had slapped him.
Then for a while she liked to watch
the black-and-yellow checkered
Cape-Cod-a-rolla in front of them
which had only been there a few months,
since the Home-a-rolla of the red-haired girl
had lost a wheel
and rolled over and over
and thrown the red-haired girl
out of the hatch and
completely out of her single rollabout.
Josette had got a horrified glimpse
of what legs and feet looked like
before the Hearse-a-rolla
scooped the girl up
and the tow truck hauled away
the mangled Home-a-rolla.
Next for a while
she always looked out the side window

at the service lane
where the Infirm-a-rolla,
the Fix-a-rolla,
the Wash-a-rolla,
and all the other mobile buildings
that served the people
rolled by in an endless rainbow circle
in the opposite direction.
And always at the last
she liked to watch
out the other side window
across the curb
beyond the chain link fence
to the endless pavement
that stretched as far as she could see.
There the great autos
(which needed no drivers)
went in any direction
swooping up and over cloverleafs
vrooming down through tunnels
or tearing along the straightaways
at five hundred miles per hour.
And sometimes,
sometimes
Josette felt a twinge of longing

that their own Home-a-rolla
just once
could vroom along the endless pavement
instead of forever sticking
to the slow and narrow home lane.

At 6 o'clock Mother always
pulled up to the Assembla-rolla
where Father adjusted
vacuum throttle positioners
to the dashpots
just as he coasted out
in his large-size rollabout.
At 6:10 Mother paused
at the Eats-a-rolla
where the supper packet
of multi-flavored Super-Cal sticks
was stuck in their food slot
and at 6:20
at the Power-rolla
where the used power unit was slid
out of the engine
and a new one slid in
and at 6:30

at the Disposa-rolla
where the filled waste unit
was replaced with an empty one.
After in-taking her calorie sticks
it was dark
and then Josette always watched
the great auto races
on the built-in Screen.
These went on and on
all day and all night
providing endless entertainment,
and now and then the Great Computer-mobile
announced the winners.
When Josette got tired she depressed
her rollabout seat
pulled up the retractable blanket
and went to sleep.

One night however
while Josette was watching
the great auto races
the Screen went blank.
The Home-a-rolla was suddenly silent
with only the thrum of its motor

and the hum of its tires on the pavement.
Josette sat shocked
for the Screen had never been
still before.
Mother turned her head.
Father rolled to the wall,
pulled out his screwdriver
and tinkered with the works
but the Screen remained empty.
Father pressed a button
on the dash and in a moment
a service truck came in the service lane,
a repairman unscrewed the Screen
and took it away.
Josette sat stupefied.
When would it be back?
What could she do
with nothing but darkness and headlights
outside
and a black hole in the wall
inside?

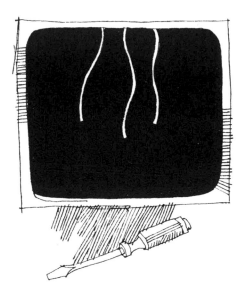

She sat for a long time.
She was not used to thinking

but a question slowly formed in her head
and even though hardly anybody ever
talked
in the Home-a-rolla
(for there was hardly ever any need to)
she asked it.
"Why can't we roll
just once
on the great-auto pavement?"
There was so long a silence
that she thought there must be
no answer,
but finally her father sputtered,
"Too dangerous!
When people
roll and vroom—
and crash
they can't be welded
like the great autos can.
So for our safety
the Great Computer-mobile –
in its infinite
wisdom
and mercy—
forbids it."

"I want a Great Person
to allow it!"
cried Josette pettishly.
"There is no Great Person,"
said her father.
Mother spoke from behind the wheel.
"There used to be a Great Person,
I think.
His name was Detroit—
and he made the first autos.
Before that there were no autos."
No autos! Josette was astonished.
"But what rolled on the endless pavement?"
"There was—
no endless pavement," said Father.
No pavement! "Then what
did Home-a-rollas and School-a-rollas run on?"
"They all stood still."
"Still!" cried Josette.
She could hardly imagine it.
All her life
except for a few seconds here and there
she had rolled on wheels
so that the very thought of standing still
made her stomach lurch.

"But how did people move?"
"They used their
legs—
first one and then the other.
It was called—
walking.
But after a while
they grew weary of
this
and so they invented autos
and pavement for the autos
to roll smoothly on.
The autos made life so very pleasant
that they built more and
more of them.
They cleared the—
land and
tore down buildings
to lay more pavement.
And then they learned to
make an auto
with a wire
cy—
cy—
cybernetic brain

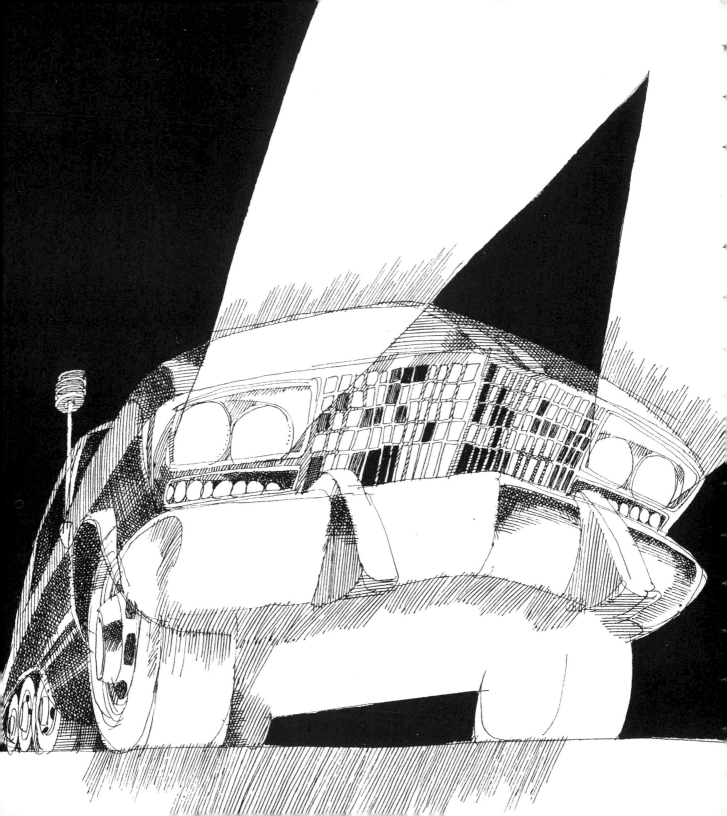

so that it could do
all the things that people did—
only better.
After that
the Great Computer-mobile
whose electronic dashboard
controls everything that moves
took over all the thinking.
It was its idea to—
keep only enough
people
for maintenance,
to put—
every person in a
rollabout
and every family
in a Home-a-rolla,
since wheels are so
much better, and—
to put Home-a-rollas in slow-speed
lanes for our protection.
Then—so that
the great autos could go everywhere
where it is necessary for them to go,
the Great Computer-mobile
bulldozed all the trees

and covered the remaining—
grass
with pavement."
"Grass?" asked Josette, puzzled.
"Trees?"
"Grass was like a soft,
green blanket
that people used to walk on
and trees—
well, trees were tall green things
like a traffic signal
studded at the top with—
calorie sticks.
People sat underneath them
to stay comfortable in summer
before there was inside Air-Kooling.
And on certain trees
I heard once from—
my father
who heard it from his father
there grew round
red things
forbidden to eat—
delicious,
but unfortunately non-fortified."

The headlights of the Great Computer-mobile
beamed at them again and announced
the winners of the last race.
Father marked them down
on his scorecard.
And then the next race began
out on the endless pavement
and the familiar noises of souped-up motors
squealing tires
and deafening crashes
filled the Home-a-rolla.
Father spoke no more.
Mother drove.
Josette depressed her rollabout seat
pulled up the retractable blanket
and tried to sleep
but her thoughts were filled
wIth grass and trees
and delicious round red things
and wishes and longings she could not name.

The next day in school
she got her bolts mixed
her wires crossed

and dropped her screwdriver so many times
that the Great Computer-mobile
from the Screen on the wall
chided her sorrowfully
and called her clumsy.
After school when she looked out
the side window
across the endless pavement
her eyes no longer saw
the green and orange and silver great autos
racing and zooming.
All that day
and the next day
and the next and the next
she watched
and wished
but she never saw what she wanted to see
or even knew for certain
what it was.

Snow fell
which melted instantly
on the No-Sno pavement
and ran off in the drains.

Then came the warmer weather
with a balmy breeze that fanned her cheek
when she steered down the home ramp
and up the school ramp.
And after a while she felt the hot wind
heavy as ten rollabout blankets
in her brief instant out-of-doors
between the Air-Kooled Home-a-rolla
and Air-Kooled School-a-rolla.
Yet still she watched and wished
though she did not drop her screwdriver
so much any more.
Then one day
she glimpsed something
partly hidden
underneath a triple cloverleaf.
Her heart leaped
like a piston.
When the Home-a-rolla came round again
a few days later
it was still there:
something green—
not quite so tall
as a traffic post;
more like the practice ones

in the Kinder-rolla driving class,
and studded with calorie sticks.
Josette watched till it was out of sight
and then she counted the hours
until she would see it again.
Sometimes the Home-a-rolla
moving in its endless circle
passed it in the morning,
sometimes in the evening,
and sometimes when she was at school
or asleep
and then she might not see it
for a week or two.
But whenever the time drew near
for the Home-a-rolla to approach it
she felt sick for fear that
the great autos would have discovered it—
but there it still was
and she was happy
for a while
until the worry set in again.
Now the wind began to nip
and one day she thought she saw
a glint of something
round and red
among the green.

Next time around
she was sure.
Josette's longing grew so fierce
she could think of nothing else
and she began to drop her screwdriver again.
Then one day
when she drove down the school ramp
she saw that they were passing by
the triple cloverleaf.
It was just a little way off
across the endless pavement!
Her heart vroomed.
At the foot of the ramp
she spun her steering wheel
and veered around
behind the Home-a-rolla
up the curb
and alongside the chain link fence.
Mother drove on
since her stops and starts
were regulated by the electronic dash
of the Great Computer-mobile.

Josette stopped
and pulled her wrench from her tool pocket.

She undid the bolts
that held her in her rollabout
and ripped back the cowling.
She pulled herself up and over the side,
slid down the hood
and crumpled onto the pavement,
for her spindle legs
had little strength in them.
She clutched the chain link fence
and hoisted herself over the top
and down the other side,
scratching herself on the wires
without even noticing.
No great autos were in sight
as she used her arms to
haul herself along the endless pavement
and after a way
she began to get the feel of her legs
so that they could help a little
in a kind of dragging crawl.
A great auto zoomed out of nowhere
and she flattened,
hoping to look like one of the crumpled fenders
that sometimes littered
the endless pavement.
The great auto sped by.

31

Now she had inched up to
the triple cloverleaf
and now she was
underneath and there it was
sticking up out of a break in the pavement:
A tree! She was sure.
With a round red thing high up
and a blanket of grass
around its base.
Her heart pounded
like a broken cam shaft.
She patted the grass and it was soft.
She touched the tree and it was rough.
She ran her hands up
as far as she could
but the round red thing
was beyond her grasping fingers.
She pulled herself to her knees
but it was still out of reach
so she held on to the little tree
and stood upright
wobbling
and now the tips of her fingers
grazed the round red thing.
She strained up on her toes

and cupped it in her hand
just as her legs buckled.
The round red thing snapped off
and she dropped to the pavement
clutching it.
It was shiny and streaky
and when she held it to her nose
it gave off such a scent
that her mouth flooded with spit
and she took a bite.
Inside it was white and crunchy
juicy and tart
like no calorie stick she had ever consumed.
She knew she would be
blissful
to go on tasting it
forever.
But as she opened her mouth
to snatch another bite
a horn blasted behind her.
She spun to see a dozen great autos
bearing down on her
and more behind them
roaring across the endless pavement

with their sirens screaming.
Before she could even cry out
a scoop truck scooped her up
and as she was carried away
she saw with anguish
a bulldozer push over the little tree
and a cement truck pour wet pavement
over the crack.

For a few moments she was having
her earliest wish,
vrooming over the pavement
around the cloverleafs and through the tunnels
at five hundred miles per hour
and then she was at the Great Garage.
The scoop truck dumped her out
and she looked up from the oily pavement
into the headlights that glared out
from beneath the severe chrome eyebrows
of the Great Computer-mobile.
Beside it was her empty rollabout.
"The clumsy one," said the Great Computer-mobile
in a reproachful purr.
"Don't you know

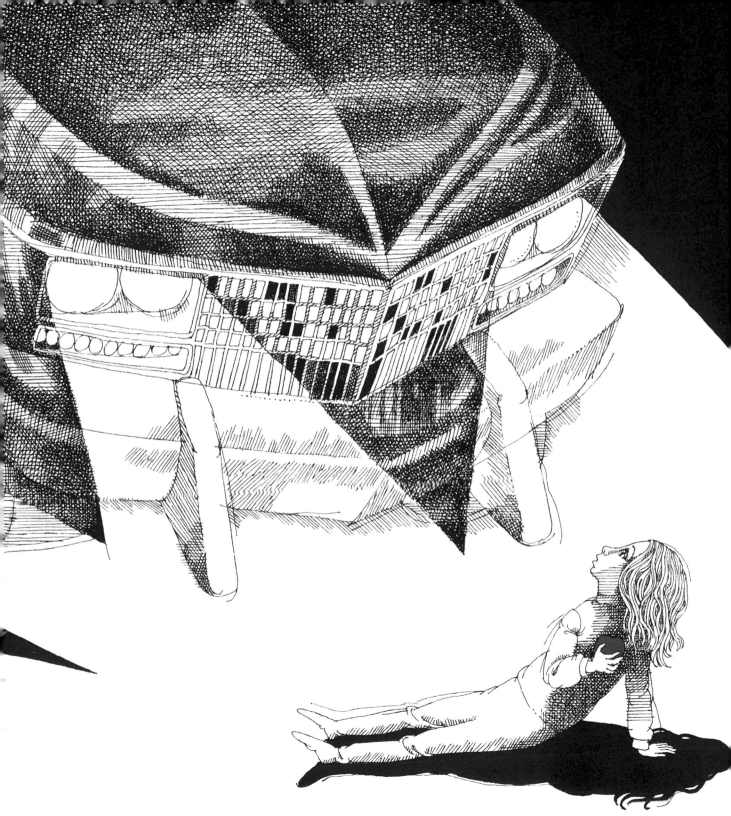

that it is for your own well-being
that I order you to stay
always in your rollabout,
and off the forbidden pavement?"
Josette was trembling so hard
that she could not answer.
Her teeth chattered
like broken gears
and tears streamed down her cheeks
like rain down a windshield
so that the Great Computer-mobile was a blur
of chrome and purple and gold.
"For such disobedience shall we take her out
and run her over?"
asked the police autos
parked on either side.
"Or shall we take her to labor
far away in the Calorie Compounds
with the others
who left their rollabouts
to try their legs?"
The Great Computer-mobile frowned.
"She is but a child
and though this is a grave offence
it is her first.

I am sure she did not fully understand
the extent of her danger.
Fit her back into her rollabout
but this time with special bolts
that only the Central Wrench can loosen
and return her to her Home-a-rolla."
It turned its brights on Josette.
"But with this warning,
clumsy one.
I will be watching,
and another offence against the great autos
will mean the Calorie Compounds—
or worse."
The Great Computer-mobile began to back
but suddenly braked.
"Wait! What is that
she has in her hand?
Get rid of it!
It is unenriched
unbalanced
and unprocessed.
Give her a nourishing Super-Cal stick
instead.
That is all."

The Great Computer-mobile turned around,
smoothly retracted its convertible top
so that Josette could see every
button and lever
dial and blinker
on its awesome electronic dash,
and rolled toward the Garage doors.
Two great autos,
their manual arms extended,
reached for Josette.
Josette found her voice.
"NO! NO!" she screeched.
"You can't have it!"
She looked around wildly
but great autos surrounded her
and there was no spot for escape.
Just as a manual arm grabbed at her hand
she flung the round thing with all her strength
after the Great Computer-mobile.
It smashed against the buttons and blinkers
and the Great Computer-mobile
stopped
with a squeal of brakes
and a scream of tires.

Josette covered her eyes in horror
because surely now
there was no hope for her.
She waited for the metal claws
to seize her
and for the dreadful purr
of the Great Computer-mobile . . .
but all was silence.
There was not even any
vroom vroom
of the great autos racing around
outside the Great Garage.
Josette peeped through her fingers.
The Great Computer-mobile was still there
stopped
and the manual arms of the great autos
their claws extended
hung motionless above her head.
All over the Great Garage
nothing stirred.
Josette lowered her hands
and thought a bit
(although it was hard work)
and then tiptoed to the purple side
of the Great Computer-mobile.

One little light on its dash
was blinking furiously.
She leaned over and loosened it
in its socket
until the light went out.
Then for good measure she took
her wrench out of her tool pocket
and hammered the entire dash
before she reached onto the seat
and picked up every fragment
of the red round thing.
Holding them carefully she wobbled
among the silent autos
to the doors of the Great Garage.
She leaned there nibbling slowly
and deliciously
while looking out at the rest of the great autos
stopped helter-skelter
as far as she could see,
and away across the chain link fence
where the Home-a-rollas
and the Service-a-rollas
stood motionless.
And as she looked
hatches began to open;

a head appeared,
and then another,
and another.
She heard a shout
and saw children
and women
and men,
their legs free,
start hunching
and somersaulting
and swinging along on their knuckles
and bumping along on their haunches
and lurching forward on all fours
up to the curb
and over the chain link fence.
Josette finished
the last juicy bite.
She tucked the core in her tool pocket
to suck on later,
collected the drip off her chin,
licked her fingers up and down,
and humming a little noise
in her throat
which she had never heard anyone
make before

she walked
to meet them all
across the endless pavement.

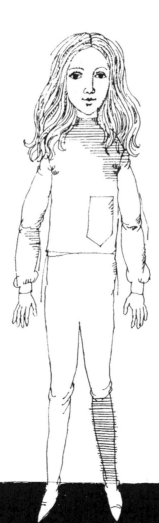